THE TRUE STORY OF THE
Three Little Pigs
and the
Big Bad Wolf

Liam Farrell
Illustrations Terry Myler

D1248553

THE CHILDREN'S PRESS

To my daughter,
Lydia Roxanne

First published 2001 by
The Children's Press
an imprint of Anvil Books
45 Palmerston Road, Dublin 6

4 6 8 7 5

© Text Liam Farrell
© Illustrations Terry Myler

ISBN 1 901737 35 7

Typeset by Computertype Limited
Printed by Colour Books Limited

Contents

There's no such word – Ed (Editor)
There is now – TBB Wolfe

How it All Began

My name is Thomas Blake-Burke Wolfe. My friends – when I had any – used to call me Tom.

Though I'm a bit down on my luck at the moment, I come from an old and honoured family. We have lived in the forest for a long, long time.

Once the name Wolfe used to mean a lot around here.

Not since I came along!

I blame it all on the Three Little Pigs and their lies. They started it. Then everyone jumped on the band-wagon.

Now I'm known everywhere as The Big Bad Wolf. People hiss and boo when I pass. *They're* the ones invited to tea at the castle and lunch with the Lord Mayor.

What happened wasn't my fault. I'm a very nice wolf really. But lately everything that happens in these parts is blamed on me. I'm the innocent victim of circumstances. That's why I want to set the record straight.

I well remember the first spot of bother I had with those three porkers. It happened shortly after they moved into the forest. They were wild right from the start, always causing trouble.

I had gone over to Red Riding Hood's cottage deep in the forest. I had heard her grandmother wasn't at all well and I thought I would take her out to lunch. Cheer her up a bit.

I'm that kind of bloke.

But as soon as I opened the front door – she keeps the key under the flower-pot on the window-sill – the crazy old biddy started to scream at the top of her voice.

'Help! Help! It's The Big Bad Wolf!'

It was the first time anyone had ever called me that. I was gobsmacked.

Try as I might, I could not stop her squealing like a Sioux Indian. In the end I thought I'd try a bit of flattery.

'My, what big eyes you have, Granny,' I cooed.

That went down like a lead balloon.

'I know what you're after,' she managed to get out, in between the screams. Her high-pitched voice left my ears ringing.

'I just wanted to have you for lunch, dear lady,' I said in a fawning voice.

That really hit the jackpot.

'Help! Help! Help! The Big Bad Wolf is going to gobble me up,' she shrieked.

I couldn't understand where I had gone wrong? Too late it hit me.

I had said: 'to have you *for* lunch.'

I had meant to say: 'to have you *out* for lunch.'

Just then, something else hit me.
Her big, heavy, frying pan.

Luckily I caught it. Otherwise it
would have sliced my head off.

I grabbed it and used it to fend off
all the other things she was throwing
at me. In between trying to duck out
through the front door.

I was half in and half out, dodging cups, saucers, plates and saucepans when who should come along, skipping and singing, but the Three Little Pigs.

Before I could explain what was happening, they dashed off to the woodcutter, who was working nearby, and told him that I was killing Little Red Riding Hood's grandmother.

Now I ask you ...

Two minutes later, this huge woodcutter turned up at full gallop, waving an axe as big as himself.

He was shouting such vile abuse that I had to shut my ears. I have never heard language like it since or before.

No way could I explain myself. I had to run for my life, fast as my legs could carry me, with this raging madman after me.

I wasn't the better of it for weeks.

Of course I told everyone the true story of what had happened.

Do you think anyone believed me?

And afterwards, that little biddy, Red Riding Hood, went around telling anyone who hadn't heard the story that I had attacked her poor old defenceless granny, and that only for the Three Little Pigs I would have gobbled her up, false teeth and all.

How nasty can you get?

HD – The Fall – *The Truth*

From that day on, it was downhill all the way.

Thomas Blake-Burke Wolfe had turned into The Big Bad Wolf.

The Three Little Pigs were all over the place, telling the sheep where I was hiding and ratting on me if I as much as looked at a hen.

That nasty Little Boy Blue threw a rotten tomato at me when my back was turned.

And Little Miss Muffet – I used to think she was such a nice child – made up a horrid rhyme about me:

> *Hide your old grannies,*
> *And lock up your fowl.*
> *Here comes Big Bad Wolfie,*
> *And he's on the prowl.*

Soon after, I came across her

sitting on a tuffet near Humpty Dumpty's house.

She was eating her lunch. A nice dish of curds and whey. Yum! Yum!

I thought now was the time to have a heart-to-heart with her and get her to stop singing that vile rhyme.

But just as I sat down beside her, a great, big, black, hairy spider fell right down before her and frightened the living daylights out of her.

Up she jumped, splashing her curds and whey all over me.

As if things weren't bad enough – Miss Muffet in hysterics, the sleeve of my new tweed jacket *ruined* with sticky curds and whey stains, and me wondering how on earth I would get them out – who should come along but the Three Little Pigs.

What do you think they did?

They started roaring, 'Help! Help! The Big Bad Wolf is attacking Little Miss Muffet.'

Then they began throwing things at me. Anything they could lay their paws on.

Sticks, stones, bits of wood and great lumps of muck. Some of them just barely missed me.

That's when the real trouble started.

Old Mr Humpty Dumpty, who is a nice pleasant sort of egg, came out of his house to see what all the fuss was about. In order to get a better view he climbed up on top of his garden wall.

When he saw what was happening he began giving those three little ruffians a right telling-off.

Then – suddenly – WHAM! He was knocked off the wall in a most vile and vicious fashion by a stone thrown by the oldest of the Three Little Pigs.

Before you could blink, all hell broke loose.

Humpty Dumpty was on the ground and all the king's horses and all the king's men were dashing about trying to put him together again.

Anyone who wasn't picking up bits of Humpty Dumpty was trying to calm Miss Muffet. Her nerves were in tatters.

Now I was in real trouble. The wrong person in the wrong place at the wrong time.

Though I had nothing to do with anything that had happened I was being blamed. And the only person who could clear me was being taken away by ambulance.

As I crawled away, a dreadful kind of chanting followed me. I paused.

Then I clearly heard the words:

What will we do with
The Big Bad Wolf?

20

I was rooted to the spot, unable to move. Then a great, flat-footed policeman came lolloping up and said, 'I'm taking you into custody for causing Serious Bodily Harm. Anything you say may be taken down and used in evidence against you. Do you wish to make a statement?'

'This is all a fiddle,' I said with dignity.

'Tell that to the judge,' he wheezed.

You may well ask why I didn't make a break for it.

Alas, by this time I was surrounded by droves of thick, flat-footed policemen. Escape was out of the question.

I Hit the Headlines

Next day, the whole affair was in the local rag, *The Daily Howl.* The Three Little Pigs' version, of course.

★ Well-known local celebrity, Mr Humpty Dumpty, was seriously injured in a civil disturbance that took place outside his home yesterday.

Eye-witness accounts place Mr TBB Wolfe, a local petty criminal, at the scene of the crime. It is understood that he is now helping police with their enquiries. Charges are expected later today.

A young lady, whose name has not yet been released, was also there but as she was taken away in a state of shock she could not be questioned.

But this newspaper can now reveal that other witnesses were present and saw what happened.

Three young brothers, who were passing that way, swear that they saw Mr TBB Wolfe creep up behind the young lady, who was sitting on a tuffet eating her lunch, and frighten her almost to death.

He then turned his attention to old
Mr Dumpty, whom he must have
thought was the only witness to his
cowardly act. It has been confirmed
by all three that Mr TBB Wolfe then
pushed Humpty Dumpty off his
garden wall.

This resulted in serious injuries to
Mr Dumpty's person. Early hospital
reports indicate that his brains have
been scrambled by the fall and he may
never be able to recall what took place
on that fateful afternoon.

While being led away, Mr TBB Wolfe was asked for a comment by our reporter at the scene, but all he would snarl was, 'Hey, Diddle Diddle.'

Police believe his accomplice, a Mr Diddle, has escaped undetected and is still at large. The public is warned that he may be armed and dangerous.

This is just another indication of the lawlessness sweeping our community. This newspaper asks where will it all stop? When will this reign of terror end? ★

Things got steadily worse from then on.

When anything happened, the police no longer said, 'Round up the usual suspects.'

They said, 'Round up the usual suspect.'

Me!

I swear I wasn't even in the meadow the day that dozey Bo-Peep lost her sheep.

How could I have been? I was in jail at the time. But naturally the police didn't get to the scene of the crime for several hours. By which time I had been seen going back to my house, having just been released on bail.

I couldn't understand why people were shouting, 'What have you done with Bo-Peep's sheep?'

But when I asked someone what the story was, the stupid yokel backed away, then fled as if for his life.

The truth about Bo-Peep and her sheep is that she spent the day messing about with her cousin, Little Boy Blue, a real pain in the neck.

The two of them had gone off to a shop on the other side of the hill for ice-cream and when they came back the sheep were gone.

They had been stampeded by Little Boy Blue and his raucous horn.
Showing off, as usual.

I heard all this later – much later – from Jack and his sister Jill who had gone up the hill to fetch a pail of water. Coming back they had this terrible accident and were taken to hospital.

So, though they saw what had happened and were prepared to speak up for me, they were unable to do so.

Indeed there were those in the village who were bad-minded enough to claim afterwards I had a hand in *their* accident as well.

Hostess from Hell

By this time my nerves were really beginning to go.

Everyone wanted to believe I was guilty of everything that happened, as this wrapped up things neatly for them.

And as for the police! They're a right shower of pigs who wouldn't recognise the truth if it jumped up and hit them.

Now I was on edge all the time. I couldn't sleep. I couldn't eat. I was a shadow of my former self. My clothes were hanging off me.

So when the Old Woman who
Lived in a Shoe, the only person who
was still talking to me, asked me to
dinner, I accepted with tears in my
eyes.

That evening I was so looking
forward to a good meal. A glass of
wine. Music. Soft lights. Someone to
whom I could pour out my heart.

What a hideous let-down!

I hadn't realised she had quite so
many children.

There were dozens of them. All
over the place. And such a tiny place.
There was scarcely room to sit down.

The less said about the meal the better.

The soup smelled delicious. Then I saw, to my horror, the Old Woman tasting it from time to time, *and putting the same spoon she had used for tasting back into the soup pot.*

My stomach curled. I knew what was lurking in that pot. Salmonella! E-coli! Listeria! Camp (something).

When it finally arrived, I had to wave it away.

The bacon must have come from a pig that died of old age. It was mainly skin – thick with stubbly bristles all over it. There was hardly any meat – just great lumps of fat and gristle.

Cabbage? It was a vile, smelly, green-coloured liquid.

The potatoes were as hard as bullets. When I tried to cut one, a segment flew off and sped like a warhead into the wall where it lodged. I tried a piece but had to give up when I felt a tooth cracking.

When I asked for a drink I was given a glass of tepid water with unidentified foreign objects floating about in it.

I was wondering what horror would follow when her mobile phone rang.

As she listened she began to back away from the table, shooing her children behind her. When she finished, she pointed at me and screamed, 'So *you're* The Big Bad Wolf. Out you go. Out! OUT!'

On the way out I was beset by those awful children, who shouted and yelled and tried to tear my clothes off.

Things Get Worse

Things, I thought to myself, could not possibly get worse.

But they did. Much, much worse.

One morning at the crack of dawn, before even the birds were out of bed, just as I was turning over on to my other side and tucking myself down snugly under the covers, it started.

At first I thought I was hearing things. There were all kinds of noises coming from outside. Hammering and banging and sawing and drilling and things.

My next thought was that maybe I was having a bad reaction to the pills the doctor had put me on for my nerves. Perhaps I should have been taking the little green ones at night instead of the little pink ones. Or maybe it should have been the big blue ones.

I was *so* confused. The noise kept getting worse. My head was splitting.

I jumped out of bed and threw back the curtains. Why my heart didn't stop then and there I'll never know. My worst nightmare was staring me in the face in the cold light of dawn. I shall never forget it as long as I live.

There they were, the Three Little Pigs, unloading all kinds of stuff from the back of a lorry. There was a sign on the top which read:

PORKY'S BUILDERS' SUPPLIERS

I knew someone wanted to build three new houses in the clearing opposite me because three notices had been put up.

No names, of course.

Naturally I objected on the grounds that this was 'contrary to the proper planning and development' of the forest and would be 'injurious to the residential amenities' of the area.

(That's the way you have to word these things – they don't speak English.)

I knew no permission had been granted – yet there they were, the Three Little Pigs, going ahead *without Planning Permission.*

'We'll see about that,' I said to myself as I grabbed my jacket. The one with the curd stains on it.

'Stop at once,' I shouted to them. 'You cannot build without Planning Permission. Desist immediately.'

'No way, Jose,' sniggered one.

'Keep your hair on, Wolfie,' twittered another, nearly flooring me with a long plank of wood. 'You don't want to get a heart attack – at your age.'

'They'll make you take them down,'
I screamed. 'This is an Illegal
Development.'

'You've got it all wrong,' sneered
the oldest pig, actually tapping me on
the chest. 'We won't have to take them
down. We'll apply for *retention*. Put
'em up first, I always say, then we'll
start talking.'

And no matter how I ranted and
raved they wouldn't stop. Oh, no!
They just kept on hammering and
banging and whistling some infernal
tune about brown paper envelopes.

At this stage I rushed into the village to see the Mayor.

Was he interested?

'Not my department,' he yawned. 'You want the Council.'

Of course the Council wasn't in. Saturday!

When I went back to the Mayor's office, he had gone. Some hanger-on, to whom I told my story, said, 'Get an injunction.'

I didn't know what *that* was but he told me to go to the Courthouse.

Closed. Saturday.

When I got back to the forest, the house of straw was up. The ones of sticks and brick were half way there.

The Three Little Pigs were lolling about.

'Hard cheese, wolfie,' giggled the oldest of the three. He was puffing a cigar. 'Take a look. You can read, can't you?'

I looked at the three notices.

Across each, in huge red lettering, were the words:

YE CAN KEEP IT
De Mare

That's the class of people running the town now. Can't spell.

The Three Little Pigs were still singing that infernal song:

> *Here's a little envelope,*
> *Beautifully brown.*
> *Stuff it full of banknotes,*
> *Build anywhere in town.*

I went home with a splitting headache.

... and Worser

When I got up in the morning, after a sleepless night, there were the three houses. All finished.

Planning? You're joking!
Bribery! Fraud! Skullduggery!
That's what I'd call it.

As my old aunt used to say, 'If you had a tune, you could sing it.'

Worse was to come.

There were three house-warming parties. Not one but three. None of which I was invited to.

Every pig in the place was there. Also Bo-Peep, Little Boy Blue, Red Riding Hood and her granny, Miss Muffet, the Three Men in a Tub, Wilken, Blinken and poor old Nod.

Not to mention the Cat and the Fiddle; he never stopped playing that squeaky thing all night. And rising above all the noise was the demented laughing of the Little Dog.

These wild parties went on until the early hours of the morning. Then there were the loud 'Good-byes' and the banging of doors. Not to mention the mess around the place afterwards. Empty crisp packets and lemonade bottles and cans everywhere.

I didn't get a wink of sleep for three whole nights.

Then they started spying on me.
THEY were always watching me and
everything I did. THEY followed me
everywhere I went. I could do nothing
but THEY were there, watching with
their sly eyes, grinning at me.

Old McDonald, whose farm was
near the forest, had some very fine
geese and every day, for the past few
weeks, he let them out for a swim in
the village pond. They had to walk
right past the back of my house on

their way to and from the pond.

They were such lovely geese, all plump and juicy. Not like those bony, skinny ones you see hanging up in supermarkets these days. I just loved to watch them waddling along.

Only that. Nothing more.

But the way THEY looked at me, you'd think I was planning to gobble them up.

As if I would. Being a vegan and all. Nothing like a cold, dry supper of nuts and lentils and pulses, I always say.

Who wants a fat tasty goose?

It wasn't only those geese.

Whenever I strolled down to enjoy the hustle and bustle of Market Day, there THEY were. Watching me like hawks. As if I had the faintest interest in all those tasty ducks and hens and chickens that would often fall off the back of a lorry.

But THEY were there, helping those silly ducks and hens and chickens back on to the carts and making vulgar signs at me.

THEY were watching me all the time.

THEY were spoiling everything.

THEY were ruining my life.

Bringing the Houses Down

It all got too much for me – and everyone knows I'm the most reasonable of wolves. I just had to put a stop to them. This was war.

All-out war.

So the very next day, after I had taken my big blue tablets, I decided to go and have it out with them. I would call around to each of their houses and give them a piece of my mind.

It was a very windy day but I put on my best coat and hat. I wanted to look like the respectable, law-abiding, honest citizen that I was.

I was hardly out through the door when my hat blew off and my coat-tails began flapping around me.

The wind was howling and the trees were swaying and branches were crashing down on top of me. I had never seen such a storm in my life.

But I gritted my teeth and struggled on. It was now or never. I had to face them and get them off my back once and for all. There was no putting it off just because of the weather.

No! That's not the way of a Thomas Blake-Burke Wolfe.

Well, by the time I arrived at the straw house I was completely goosed. The wind had now risen to *gale force nine* and I could hardly breathe. I had to huff and puff to get some air into my lungs. As for keeping my balance – it was impossible.

I staggered up to the front door and literally fell against it, still huffing and puffing.

Suddenly, the whole house fell in.

I swear I had nothing to do with it. It just fell in. Collapsed in a heap on the ground.

I know it sounds hard to believe but it shows what will happen when you let amateurs build a house with inferior materials.

And without Planning Permission.

Now there was just a great big pile of straw blowing around in the wind, and what do I see but the youngest of the Three Little Pigs, his tail stuck up in the air, running across the back yard to his brother's house, shouting at the top of his voice.

'Help! Help! Let me in! Let me in! The Big Bad Wolf has blown my house down.'

Of course this was all nonsense!

But what was I to do? I felt I just had to go round to brother number two and explain to him what had really happened.

So, wrapping my coat tightly around me, I set off towards his house. The one made of sticks. A fine house it was too, with velux windows in the roof and a deck where he used to sit in the evenings and look right into my sitting-room.

By this time the wind was really
howling about my ears. *Gale force ten.*
I was still finding it hard to breathe as
I knocked on the second door.

This loud voice demanded, 'Who is
it?'

Now just how silly can you get.

Of course it was me.

I tried to answer but I was huffing
and puffing so much that I couldn't.

I knocked again – and you won't
believe this!

The whole house fell in.

I swear I had done nothing but knock twice on the door.

Next thing I know the whole house is around my ankles and two little pigs are running across the garden towards the oldest brother's house. The one I might add who did the mischief to poor old Humpty Dumpty.

And they're shouting at the tops of their voices, 'Help! Help! Let us in. Let us in. The Big Bad Wolf has blown both our houses down.'

Of course that was a lie. A total lie if ever I heard one. I did *not* blow either of their flimsy houses down.

I was very upset by these lies. So I marched over the oldest pig's house, the one made of bricks, and banged on his front door. I was determined to have a word with the three of them.

To put the record straight. I wanted to get this over with now, this minute.

I was just about to bang on the door again when a slate, lifted by the wind, fell off the roof and knocked me senseless on the ground.

The next thing I knew, I was being carted away by the police on two counts of Breaking and Entering and of causing Criminal Damage to Private Property owned by two of the Three Little Pigs.

Those honest upright citizens!

They told the police I had huffed and puffed and blown two of their houses down, and only that the third was made of bricks I would have blown it down as well.

Now here I am, locked up in a cold damp jail, waiting for my case to come before the court.

PS. Be sure not to miss the sequel, *The Trial of the Big Bad Wolf.*

See you in court!

Hello, there!

Let me tell you about a new series of books called **Elephants**.

Do you know anything about elephants? That we're very very wise? And live a very very long time? And we never forget anything – ever?

So **Elephants** are like me – wise, last a long time and you'll never forget them.

Sounds like the right name to me.

One day I'll be the biggest animal in the jungle. But right now I want to tell you a lot of stories. I've chosen them myself. We'll have lots of fun reading them.

They're *so* easy to read. Short words

mostly. Short sentences. Lots of
illustrations. Lots of jokes.

TIPS

I'm a second-stage reader but I find
long words difficult. But I have a very
smart cousin called Homer. His tip?
Break it up. If you see a word like
'circumstances', don't panic. Take it
apart: cir - cum - stances .
Isn't that easier?

'Everywhere' is every - where .
'Wondering' is won - der - ing .
Reading is easy the
Elephant way.

Elephants – easy reading for new readers who have moved on a stage. Still with –

Large type
Mostly short words
Short sentences
Lots of illustrations
And fun!

This is the first **Elephant.**
Look out for more.

Liam Farrell lives in Maynooth, Co Kildare. He has one daughter, Lydia.

He writes short stories and articles for magazines and newspapers. This is his first children's book. The sequel is *The Trial of the Big Bad Wolf.*

Terry Myler, one of Ireland's best-known illustrators, has also written *Drawing Made Easy* and *Drawing Made Very Easy.*